Ready, Set, Tow!

Adapted by Mary Tillworth

Based on the teleplay "The Pickle Family Campout"
by Veronica Pickett and Clark Stubbs

Illustrated by Heather Martinez

A GOLDEN BOOK • NEW YORK

© 2018 Viacom International Inc. All rights reserved. Published in the United States by Golden Books, an imprint of Random House Children's Books, a division of Penguin Random House LLC, 1745 Broadway, New York, NY 10019, and in Canada by Penguin Random House Canada Limited, Toronto. Golden Books, A Golden Book, A Little Golden Book, the G colophon, and the distinctive gold spine are registered trademarks of Penguin Random House LLC. Nickelodeon, Nick Jr., Blaze and the Monster Machines, and all related titles, logos, and characters are trademarks of Viacom International Inc.

rhcbooks.com
ISBN 978-1-5247-6843-0
T#: 556698
Printed in the United States of America
10 9 8 7 6 5 4 3 2 1

Blaze and AJ were zooming through the forest when they suddenly heard singing. They followed the sound to a campsite full of happy green trucks!

"Welcome to the Pickle Family Campout!" the trucks cheered.

"These are my cousins, Ben, Ken, and Sven," Pickle told Blaze. "And over there picking flowers are my sisters, Lily, Millie, Tillie, and Frilly!"

Pickle's grandpa appeared—with Crusher hanging from his fishing line!

"You'll never believe what I caught," he said. "A big blue fish!"

"Silly Grandpa!" Pickle laughed. "You forgot to wear your glasses!"

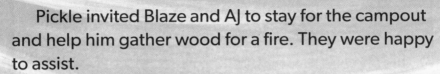

Pickle invited Blaze and AJ to stay for the campout and help him gather wood for a fire. They were happy to assist.

"Crusher, do you want to help, too?" Pickle asked.

"No way!" he sniffed.

Pickle grinned. "Then you get the most important job: taking care of my little brother, Baby Gherkin!"

Blaze, AJ, and Pickle rumbled through the forest in search of logs.

Pickle saw a fallen tree. "This is perfect for a campfire!"

But when Pickle tried to move it, he lost his balance and toppled over the edge of a cliff!
"Uh-oh. Blaze? Help!" he cried.

Blaze knew how to rescue Pickle. "I need to turn into the ultimate pulling machine: a tow truck!" he said. "First, we need a cable with a hook. Next, we need a telescoping boom to move the cable up and down. Finally, we need a winch to give us super pulling power."

When all the parts came together, Blaze transformed into . . . Tow-Truck Blaze!

Blaze flung his hook down to Pickle. With all his might, he pulled Pickle back onto solid ground! Pickle dusted himself off. "Finding firewood sure is hard. I hope the rest of my family is doing okay."

Ring! Ring!
Pickle's cousins were calling. They were trapped in tickling spiderwebs!

Ring! Ring!
Pickle's sisters were calling, too. They were lost in a swamp!

Ring! Ring!
Now Pickle's grandpa was calling. Without his glasses, he had wandered into a volcano!
"Tow-Truck Team to the rescue!" said Blaze.

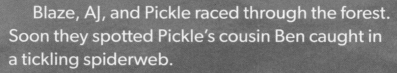

Blaze, AJ, and Pickle raced through the forest. Soon they spotted Pickle's cousin Ben caught in a tickling spiderweb.

"We can't possibly break a web that strong," Pickle said.

"Oh yes we can—with a heavy load!" declared Blaze. "A load is how much weight something is holding. If we add more things to the web, the load will get heavier and heavier, until—*snap!* The web breaks!"

Blaze tossed a shovel into the web. Combined with Ben's weight, the load was heavy enough to break the strands. Blaze grabbed Ben with his tow hook and pulled him free!

Pickle saw his cousin Ken stuck in another web.
He threw some paddles into it to make a heavier load.
He saved his cousin!

Sven was caught in a different web. Blaze threw in
a frying pan and a flashlight, but the load still wasn't
heavy enough.

Pickle had an idea. "Blaze, I'm pretty heavy. You can
throw *me*!"

Blaze tossed Pickle into the web, and the two trucks
tumbled free.

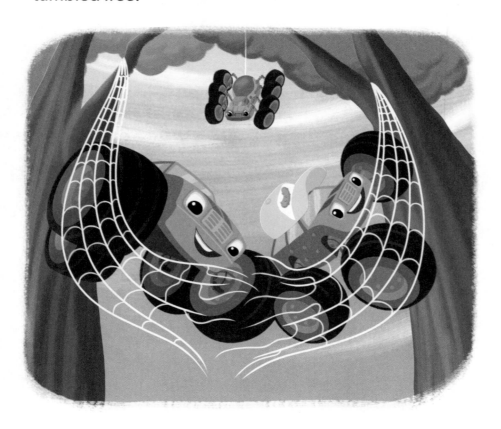

Blaze, AJ, Pickle, Ben, Ken, and Sven hurried through the forest. They came upon a foggy swamp. "My sisters!" Pickle shouted. "They're floating away!"

"Hang on!" Tow-Truck Blaze flung his hook into the water and pulled Pickle's sisters to safety, one by one.

Pickle was as relieved as they were.

"Come on, Tow-Truck Team," Blaze said. "Let's go get Grandpa!"

Blaze, AJ, and Pickle and his family rushed to find Grandpa. Soon they reached a volcano.

"Grandpa must be in here!" said Pickle. He headed inside with Blaze and AJ. They saw Grandpa on the other side of a huge pit of boiling lava!

Pickle noticed some pointy rocks dangling from the ceiling. "I'm coming, Grandpa!" He threw his hook around one of the rocks and tried to swing over. But he was too heavy. With a *crack*, the rock broke loose!

Blaze used his hook to snag Pickle in the nick of time.

"That rock couldn't carry your load," Blaze told Pickle. "To save Grandpa, we need to find rocks that are strong enough to swing on."

Blaze saw one that looked like it could support a heavy load. He grabbed Pickle and latched his tow hook onto the rock. They were ready to swing over to Grandpa!

Blaze, AJ, and Pickle swung from rock to rock, making sure each one could hold their load. They were slowly getting closer to Grandpa—but now the volcano was about to erupt!

With a final swing, Blaze, AJ, and Pickle soared over the lava and reached the other side. Pickle grabbed Grandpa, and Blaze flipped back over the pit, carrying everyone to safety!

The Pickle Family Campout was on! Back at the campsite, everyone enjoyed toasted marshmallows over a roaring fire—especially new friends Baby Gherkin and Crusher!